About the Author

This is her second book, and she cannot stop writing. At the age of sixty-four, she has lived a full life and finally has time to pursue her passion of writing. She started with poems, mostly of the amusing variety, and then decided to delve into the world of storytelling. Hailing from the land of poets and scholars, Eire, she hopes that the literary culture of her homeland is rubbing off on her.

She has always loved reading, especially as an escapism from the ups and downs of life. A book had to capture her interest from the first line, and her hope is to do the same for her readers.

The Dungeon

Ann K. S. Thayre

The Dungeon

Olympia Publishers
London

www.olympiapublishers.com
OLYMPIA PAPERBACK EDITION

A CIP catalogue record for this title is
available from the British Library.

ISBN: 978-1-80439-668-1

This is a work of fiction.
Names, characters, places and incidents originate from the writer's
imagination. Any resemblance to actual persons, living or dead, is
purely coincidental.

First Published in 2024

Olympia Publishers
Tallis House
2 Tallis Street
London
EC4Y 0AB

Printed in Great Britain

Dedication

I dedicate this book to my sister, Barbara, who is also my best friend.

Acknowledgements

Thank you to everyone who has been encouraging me to keep going and to aim higher. There are too many to mention and in fear of leaving one out, I am sure you all know who you are.

Chapter 1

I tried to move my head, but it felt like a million explosions. Tentatively I opened my eyes. All I could see was a faded white ceiling. I could hear distant noises, but I couldn't make out what they were.

Gradually as the banging in my head subsided, I began to turn my head from side to side very slowly.

Taking in my surroundings didn't take long as I seemed to be in a dirty room and there was an awful smell of dampness.

I heard some footsteps coming closer. There wasn't much light in the room. There was a door to my left, and, as I turned, it slowly opened. I could just make out a shape, and, as it moved towards me, the banging in my head began again and everything went black.

I don't know how long I had been passed out for but the next time I came to, the banging in my head wasn't as loud and I was able to move a little bit easier. Opening my eyes again, I could see a small light coming from a single bulb in the corner of the room. I tried to sit up but as I began to move my leg, a shearing pain went through me, and the room went black again.

The next time I woke up, the banging in my head had all but gone. I pulled myself into a sitting position, wincing and crying with pain. Looking down at my leg, I could see a big gash, and my leggings were torn. The movement had started it bleeding but looking around, I couldn't see anything I could use as a bandage. With a great deal of effort, I moved my leg over the side of the bed followed by the other leg. As I sat there breathing heavily and sweating, I tried to remember how I had gotten there. When my heartbeat slowed again, I tried to stand up, but I got a sharp pain in my leg and head. Feeling dizzy, I dropped back down on the bed sobbing. It was obvious, my leg needed some support. I ripped the remains of the leggings leg and tied it tightly around the wound. I felt instant relief.

As my eyes became accustomed to the light, I was able to make out some objects in the room. There was a bucket with a toilet roll on the floor beside it. Feeling the urge to use it, I wasn't sure if I would be able to make it over to where it was. There was a table close to the bed, and I reached forward to try and hold onto it. My fingertips just touched the edge of the table, and I fell back on the bed with exhaustion. Taking a deep breath, I pulled myself up into the sitting position again, thanking the lucky stars that I had been attending the gym regularly. This time, I pulled myself closer to the edge of the bed and stretching hard I was just about able to reach the table. Grabbing it as best I could, I pulled it towards me to a point where I could get both hands on it. Taking a deep breath and holding tight, I pulled myself up to stand. I waited for the pain to subside and the room to stop spinning. The distance to the bucket seemed farther away but I shuffled along the floor slowly holding the table. When I got to the end of the table, there seemed to be the same distance to the bucket. Fortunately, the table was not heavy. I edged around it until I had my back to the bucket. Taking small steps backwards, I pulled the table after me. It seemed to take forever. Before I reached the point where I could drop my clothes and hold onto the table, I sat on the bucket. Looking down, I could see blood had reached my socks and it dawned on me that I had no shoes. Where were my shoes?

I made the reverse journey back to the bed a lot more slowly, and collapsed into a heap.

Chapter 2

I awoke to the smell of food. Pulling myself into a sitting position, I could see a plate of food on the table and beside it a tumbler that looked like it had water in it. As I stood, I could see it was a paper plate with a congealed egg on it alongside two slices of bread. A sliced-up brown apple was also on the plate and the overall appearance showed it had been there a while. But as my stomach gave a loud grumble, I didn't care. I peeled the egg off the plate bringing some paper with it; I slapped it between the bread and took a bite. Not the Savoy but at least it would give me some strength. The apple was very sour, and I washed it down with the metallic-tasting water. As I ate, I saw a first aid kit had been left. No scissors of course, but at least I would be able to clean my leg.

A while later feeling a little sated and my leg cleaned, I took better stock of my surroundings. There wasn't a window, just the door and the bulb. Apart from the table and the bed, there was no furniture. I couldn't tell what time of day or night it was and with that, the light went out.

I lay back on the bed hoping sleep would take me quickly.

Something had woken me up and I lay staring into the darkness. Noises from above sounded dull and I was unable to decipher what they were. Suddenly the light came on, and I heard a noise at the door. Sitting up straight, I waited with a pounding heart to see who came in. As the door opened slowly, I held my breath. A shape filled the doorway, but it had a hood over its head. It didn't speak so I had no way of knowing if it was a man or a woman. Carrying a tray to the table, I wondered if I could make a dash for it but thought better of it as my leg was still painful. Better to wait and try to find out what was going on or even where I was.

'Who are you? What do you want with me? Where am I? Speak to me please,' I begged.

There was no reply. After depositing the food on the table, they walked out. Next time, I would focus more on their shape and movement to see if I could make out if it was a man or a woman.

It looked like a plate of breakfast. It must be morning. I ate the dried bread slowly and washed it down with the lukewarm tea.

With nothing to do, I lay back on the bed and fell asleep. Waking later again and not knowing what time it was, I decided to try to keep mobile. With effort, I stood up and rested on the table. Holding on with one hand and using the other for balance, I shuffled around the table; despite the pain, I circled it four times before collapsing on the bed again drifting into a sleep.

The sound of the door opening again woke me. It looked like the same person carrying the tray.

'What time is it? Can you bring me something to read and wet wipes, please?' I begged them.

There was no reply, and the figure left the room.

This time, the food consisted of a mug of soup and a banana without its skin. Did they think I would leave the skin on the floor for them to slip on? Maybe if I mashed up the banana and spread it on the floor that would work. But I was too hungry and ate it. The soup had no flavour, but it was hot which I suppose was a bonus.

As I exercised shuffling around the table, I hoped that the food was lunch as that would mean there would be dinner. This would help to orientate me to what time of day it was, and I could start trying to add up the days.

Chapter 3

Using my fingernail, I had managed to scratch a mark on the table for every day I thought I had been there. So far twelve days that I was aware of had gone by.

Although I remembered everything about myself, it was how I got there that eluded me. I kept going over my routine. It must have been a Saturday as I had gone on my run early. On workdays, I did it at lunchtime. I had left the house with my bottle of water, my Fitbit on, and music playing through my headphones. I now understood why it was not advisable to wear headphones as you cannot hear anyone coming close to you. I remember reaching the little bridge over the stream in the park and stopping to drink my water – no it wasn't water it was an energy drink. I remember I had been feeling very tired recently and thought it would help me complete the run. The sun had not yet risen enough to dry the dew off the bridge and as I stood there and finished my drink, I thought it would be a beautiful day. And that was where it went blank and no matter how hard I tried I couldn't remember anything until I woke up in this room. I must have been drugged – but how?

My request for books had been answered. Although none of them had ideas about escape, I enjoyed reading most of them. In fact, I am sure a couple of them came from my house. It occurred to me that they must have been in the house, but was it before or after my kidnap? I shivered as I realised they could have been watching me for a long time.

The food hadn't improved but at least I could freshen up with the wipes. My hair felt dirty and itchy, and my clothes must be smelling. A shower would be wonderful right now.

I had been studying the body movements of my captor and decided it was a man. I worked out that he was about 6'4" and he was quite wide on the shoulders. I guessed this from lining him up with a mark on the door and then standing beside it. I was 5'7"; and standing next to the mark, I was able to guess at his height. He had big feet and always wore slippers. The boiler suit and hood covered everything. I could not see his eyes as he wore sunglasses. Imagine the sort of description I would give the police if I ever got out of here!

Chapter 4

Day thirteen and my leg seemed to have healed. A crust had formed, but it should have been stitched, and it would be scarred. It was time to come up with a plan to get out. But what could I do? There wasn't a chair to hit him over the head with. The bed was moulded so nothing could be broken off. That left the bucket, which was plastic and wouldn't do any damage, and the table.

I examined the legs of the table, and although they were screwed on, I thought if I put enough effort into it, I might be able to get one off or even lay the table on its side and break one. But then what? It would immediately be noticed that the table was uneven. Would there be enough books to stack up and balance the table? Maybe if I rested the table against the bed, it would work.

The light went out, and I drifted off, dreaming about whacking people over the head with books!

It was still dark when I next woke up. I felt refreshed but, without the light, there was no way of knowing what time of night it was. Unable to read in the dark, I lay there continuing to plan. My stomach started to grumble, it must be near morning. I went to the door to try and listen but could not hear anything. Out of habit, I tried the doorknob not expecting it to give but to my surprise, it began to turn.

My brain could not engage the knowledge that the knob was turning, and I stood looking at it. I gave myself a shake and turned the knob slowly. I eased the door towards me and crept out. There was no sound. I stepped into what looked like a cellar or in my imagination, a dungeon. There was a very small window near the ceiling with daylight streaming through. I ran and stood in the beam of light feeling its warmth while I looked around. There was a flight of steps on the other side of the room and with a deep breath, I went as fast and as quietly as I could up to the top of them. The door at the top was slightly ajar and I edged it open further. Stepping through, I found myself in the ruins of a building. It was open to the elements and looked black as though there had been a fire. I could hear pigeons but that was the only sound.

I decided to follow what looked like a path through the debris to the remains of an entrance. Having no shoes, I could feel every bit of stone and dirt on the soles of my feet, I tried to be careful whilst also trying to be fast. Looking out the entrance, I saw fields but no other buildings. There were car tracks leading away down a driveway, I hobbled along these as it was a bit easier on my feet. By the time I reached the main gate – which was open – I was limping badly and breathing extremely heavily. Resting my hands on my knees to recover, I noticed my leg was bleeding. Lifting my feet one by one, I saw blood on my socks. I didn't think I could get far with my injuries, but I had to try. Looking left and right there was nothing but a road with trees on either side of it. I turned left and began to run as best I could.

I was at the point of exhaustion, with sweat and blood dripping when I saw a dot in the distance coming closer. Realising it was a car, I did not know whether to hide or take a chance and flag it down. I waited until I could see that it was a mini car with a driver. With relief and a lot of hope, I lifted my arm to wave. I felt a sharp pain, and everything went black.

19

Chapter 5

When I awoke, I was back in the room and the light was on. As my head cleared, I felt something beside me in the bed. Moving as quickly as I could, I stood up. When my head calmed down, I looked closely at the shape. Pulling back the cover, I could see it was a young woman. Her long blonde hair was matted with blood. I could see her chest rise and fall, therefore I knew she was not dead. All I could do was cover her up and wait.

My stomach began to rumble. I had not eaten all day and as the light went out, all I could do was lie on the bed again and sleep.

When I opened my eyes, the light was on, and there was food on the table. Cold sausage and beans alongside a big mug of cold tea. There was also a note that read, *Try that again and you will be sorry.*

My stomach knotted, and I felt defeated. As tears streamed down my face, I made a decision; I would not give up.

Hearing a moan, I looked at the girl. She was coming round. 'Where am I?' she asked.

'I don't know. But try not to move too quickly as you have a gash on your head. When you can sit up, I will have a look at it and try to clean it.'

'Are you hungry? You can have a sausage and half of the beans, and I left you half of the tea.' She shook her head slowly.

'You have to eat as I have been working on a plan to get out.'

I realised she was crying so I sat on the bed beside her,

putting my arm around her shoulder.

'What is your name?' I asked. 'I'm Rachel.'

'I'm Susanna,' she replied. 'How did I get here? What do they want?'

'I don't know. I have been here over two weeks, maybe longer, and no one has spoken to me. Here, drink your tea, and I will start cleaning our wounds.'

My feet were scratched and bleeding, and, using my teeth, I tore the bandage in half and tied them around my feet. Next, I repatched my leg using the dirty bit of legging to hold the gauze in place. I looked at Susanna.

'I'm going to check your head.' Parting her hair, I could see a gash. It didn't look too bad but there was a lump. I cleaned it with the remains of the wipes and hoped that would be enough. Susanna curled up on the bed and went back to sleep.

My feet were so painful I was unable to do my routine walks around the table. There was nothing for it but to lie down and try to get some more rest.

A piercing scream cut into my sleep. Susanna was sitting bolt upright and looking at the door. The kidnapper was standing in the doorway looking at us. He backed out, closing the door again.

I held Susanna while she cried. 'Can you remember anything about how you got here?' I prompted her to think. There could be some clues in her story to give us an indication as to why we were here.

'I cannot really remember. One minute I was in a pub, and the next I was here. I had gone out with some friends who – when the pub was closing – decided to go into town to a club. I didn't want to go and went into the ladies. I remember leaning over the sink to splash some water on my face, the sound of the door opening, and then waking up here. It's a blank.' And she began to sob.

I thought it was definite then; we had both been drugged. Neither of us had been assaulted, as far as we were aware. So, the question remained: Why?

I thought back to the car on the road and told Susanna about it. Hopefully, I had been seen by the driver, but would they have realised what was happening?

Susanna had gone back to sleep, so I read for a while. The light went out. No dinner tonight then.

Chapter 6

The light came on, and another day began. Susanna looked a little better, and we waited for the food to arrive. As time went on and no food arrived, we began to wonder what was happening. We were very thirsty, and our stomachs took turns to grumble loudly. We talked a lot about who we were, what we did, our families, and anything we could think of to pass the time. It made our mouths dry, and there was no water, so we stopped.

We lay on the bed, waiting for the light to go out, but it didn't. Were they trying to confuse us? We couldn't tell now if it was day or night. No food was brought, and we were beginning to panic. We kept trying the door and banging on it, but I knew it was hopeless. We were in a room below a ruin. There was no one to hear us.

Time went on, and we began to get weaker without food and drink. We slept on and off, feeling very disoriented. The bucket was full, but it didn't matter. Without food and water, we wouldn't be needing it.

We lay on the bed, holding hands as we became weaker and weaker. The bulb had flickered a few times, and we hoped it wouldn't go out. Susanna was the first to slip into a coma, and I knew I would not be far behind. I kept hold of her hand. It gave me comfort to know I wasn't going to die on my own.

I was dreaming. I could see masks. Strange people looking at me, poking at me. I drifted in and out. I could hear screaming but could not focus on where it was coming from. The nightmares went, and it was dark again.

I tried to open my eyes, but they felt heavy. Someone touched my hand, and I tried to scream but nothing came out.

As I forced my eyes open while thrashing around, a figure came into focus. Then a man in a white coat jabbed my arm, and I drifted off again.

Waking later, the same woman was by my bed, and I realised she was a nurse. She held my hand. 'Now, hush, dear. You are safe now.'

'Who are you? Where am I?' I croaked as she held a glass of water to my lips.

As I sipped the water, she told me she had seen me on the road a few days beforehand and not thought anything of it.

'As I drove past, I saw a man gather you in his arms, and it looked like you were both having a romantic cuddle.' It was not until about two days later I was watching the news, and an announcement was made about another young woman who had gone missing in the area. I didn't think much of it at first as she was described as having blonde hair. Later at work, I saw a different news station, and it covered the story about you being missing. It then registered that it was you I had seen. I immediately called the police, and a search began. I expect the police will want to speak to you soon. They have been waiting. Do you feel up to it?'

As I drifted off again, I heard her say, 'I guess not.'

Chapter 7

The next time I woke up, there was a female PO sitting by the bed reading. I watched her for a few minutes. I tried to speak, but my mouth was dry. She heard me and looked up. Without saying anything, she got me a glass of water and rang the bell for the nurse.

The nurse came in and raised me up in the bed. She went away again saying she would be back with something for me to eat.

I looked at the PO and asked if Susanna was all right.

'Please call me Jo, and, yes, she is doing okay. We got to you both just in time. Another day, and it might have been a different story.'

'What happened? How did you find us?'

'Please understand that I cannot tell you too much detail as a case is being built against the perpetrators and we want nothing to get in the way of bringing them to justice. We are still unsure if it was a gang or an individual.

'The woman in the car, as you know, is a nurse and was returning from a night shift. She spotted you ahead with your arm half raised. A man was behind you and swung you around to face him. As she drove past, he had his head bent towards you and she thought you were kissing. He had blonde hair which had dropped over his face, so she did not get a good look at him. She just thought you were having a "romantic" moment. She said that she thought, "how lovely to have a tall man to look up to". She carried on, and, as she told you, when she saw your story on the news, she came to see us. At first, we thought it unlikely you would be out in broad daylight, but when we put the report to the investigating team, they were excited.

'They had been investigating a gang of people traffickers, and although the description was vague, they had a blonde tall man in their sights.'

I interrupted her, 'I find this hard to believe. Don't traffickers bring people into the country, not out of it?'

Jo sat back in her chair. 'Oh, you would not believe what they get up to. It is not only kidnapping girls for arranged marriages, but now with the terrorist groups, they want foreign women to prove a point to the world that they can get in under the radar and disrupt our way of life.

'This particular group has been working out of Amsterdam, and we have the Dutch police tracking them from Holland. It seems they get as far as Russia, and because we cannot always follow them into Russia, we lose track of them.'

She hesitated for a moment, letting the news sink in.

'I will go and get us a drink if you like before I continue.'

'Yes, please,' I croaked. I was shaking with the realisation I had had a lucky escape.

Jo came back with two mugs of coffee. 'The nurse made them in the kitchen; they are nice and hot and taste better than from the machine. Do you want me to carry on?' she asked, putting the mug down on the tray over the bed.

I nodded, wrapping my hands around the mug, gaining some comfort from the warmth.

'Well,' Jo began again, 'the detective in charge of the case got permission to launch a drone over the area. It took some arranging. They spotted the ruins among the trees and a van parked. Thinking this was unusual, they took aerial photos and had them superimposed. It resembled a van they had been looking for, but they couldn't tell for sure as they couldn't read the number plates. After studying the pictures for a while, they sent the drone back up. It stayed up as long as they could keep it there, and, eventually, their patience paid off. They finally got to see the blonde man. However, they could not work out where he was going to and coming from in the ruins, and they couldn't take the drone lower.

Eventually, they took a chance and had the van followed while they sent a search and rescue team in to search the ruins. Nothing was found. They had left no traces of anything.'

I lay back on the pillow with my eyes closed thinking about how close we had come to not being found.

Jo continued, 'The DCI decided to get some fresh eyes to look at the photos. They called in a local architect, and he brought a local estate agent with him. Between them, they were able to make out the house they were looking at. There had been a fire about fifty years earlier, and the whole family died in it. It has remained a ruin ever since. They did suggest there could be a cellar, and sometimes the big houses had a room built off the cellars for extra cold storage. However, the photos did not give any clues.'

I could feel myself drifting off. Jo stood up and said she would finish in the morning.

I stopped her. 'I need to know now how you found us.

With a sigh, she sat back down, and, taking a breath, she continued, 'The DCI sent a new team, and this time they took heat-seeking equipment and dogs. Believe it or not, it was the dogs that sniffed you out. They had already examined the cellar previously, but the door to the room off the cellar was very well camouflaged. That is all I know at this point.'

'Did they catch him?' I wanted to know.

'The van was followed to a warehouse on the seafront, and, yes, they caught a man. As I said, I cannot tell you details.'

I burst into tears, and she reached forward and took my hand.

'You are safe here, but we are waiting for news from Holland to find out if they have been successful on their end. In the meantime, there is a policeman outside your door so try not to worry.'

I told her to go; I needed to be on my own. When she left, I curled up in a ball and cried myself to sleep.

Chapter 8

The next day, with the help of the nurse, I was able to walk around the room. I looked out over the town wondering how many other girls and women were at risk. I thought about Susanna and asked the nurse how she was doing. At that moment, the door opened and there she was in a wheelchair being pushed by a nurse. I shuffled over and gave her a long hug. We both cried.

Helping me back to the bed, the nurses left us alone. I told Susanna the story the PO had told me. She was horrified and said out loud what I was afraid to face.

'We are still in danger; they could still get us,' she screamed. The duty police officer rushed in followed by the nurses who knelt beside Susanna to comfort her.

My heart was racing. She was right and where did it leave us and our lives? Until these people were caught, we would remain in danger.

When Susanna stopped crying, she asked if it was possible that we could be put in a room together. The nurses thought this would be okay, and, later in the day, another bed was wheeled in with Susanna in it. At the same time, Jo, the police officer, came in, followed by a man. He was quite stocky and had an air of authority about him. He introduced himself as DCI Jones, the DCI in charge of the case. I noticed he had a very warm smile and greyish eyes. He asked us to go over our stories again which we did, this time Jo recorded everything that was being said.

When we had finished, I asked if the gang had been caught yet. The DCI and Jo exchanged glances. Then looking at us, he said they had missed them. Although they had staked out the warehouse, the blonde man had not returned nor had anyone else. All they could do now was wait to see what the Dutch turned up.

Susanna shouted, 'But what is to happen to us while you wait? We could still be in danger.'

Jo put her arms around her to calm her down. DCI Jones explained that they would be kept in the hospital until they were fit to go home. At every point, they would have a police officer with them. There would also be one on duty outside the apartment.

With a touch of sarcasm, I said I hoped they could run.

DCI Jones looked at me with soft eyes and nodded his head. 'I understand how you must be feeling. You both have been through an ordeal, and I can assure you, we will do everything to protect you.'

I did not feel reassured, and I could see Susanna wasn't either.

When they left, Susanna said she wanted to ask me something. I was very tired and rubbing my forehead; I told her to ask away.

'Can I stay with you when we get out of here? I don't want to go back to my parents in case it puts them in danger, and, besides, I would feel better knowing that you would be around. We could watch out for each other. What do you think?

'Let me think about it. I am sorry, but I feel exhausted and want to sleep. Good night.'

Before she settled down, Susanna checked the policeman was still outside the door. She was very anxious.

I lay in the dim light thinking how it would work. I really

didn't want to go back to my apartment knowing strangers could have been in there without me knowing. But, at this moment, I did not have much choice, and maybe Susanna being there would help. Another set of eyes and ears. I could ask the police to get the locks changed before we moved back in.

Chapter 9

The next morning, I asked the duty policeman to tell the DCI that I wished to speak to him.

Later in the day, DCI Jones arrived bearing gifts. 'Thought you girls would like some chocolates.' He put a box on each of our beds. 'Now what did you wish to talk to me about?'

I asked him if there was a chance we could go into protective custody as we were feeling frightened to return home. When he said no, I explained that I would like the locks changed on my apartment, and Susanna would be moving in with me until the gang was caught.

The DCI put his hands in his pockets, and, looking down at the floor, waited a couple of minutes before he spoke.

'I think it is a good idea to be together. I am sure there would be no objection to using the budget to have the locks changed. However, we will be unable to change the one into the main building. You will have to remain vigilant, but, as we said yesterday, there will be a PO with you.'

'Great,' I said. 'When you have changed the locks, let the hospital know and we can arrange to leave here, please.'

He nodded and left the room.

The rest of the day was quiet. Susanna's parents came to visit. Friends were not allowed. My parents had died a year earlier, and, being an only child, there were no visitors for me. This suited me because I could sit and think about all the activities I was involved in and whether doing them would put me in danger again. Would the gang try to kidnap me again?

The following day, DCI Jones and Jo arrived. They handed us each a mobile phone and a set of keys.

'The locks are done. The phones have trackers in them, so we know where you are, and our numbers have been put in. We don't expect you to have to use it, but we have set the emergency number to come straight to our incident room, where someone will be there to answer twenty-four hours a day. All you must do is press and hold for at least five seconds. Have you got any questions?'

We shook our heads.

'Right,' Jo said, 'the hospital will discharge you later, and we will send a car for you. I will try to be in it. In the meantime, if you think of anything you want to know or remember, please phone me.' They left the room giving reassuring smiles as they went.

Later that day, after lunch, the nurse came in and changed my dressings on my feet.

'I would give them another day covered, and then you can take the bandages off. Your leg is healing nicely, and we will have you back in a week to check on the stitches. I'm afraid you will be left with a scar, but we did the best we could for you. I am going off duty soon, so I wish you both well and look after each other.'

I thanked her, and, as she left, a doctor came in.

'Here are your discharge papers and your painkillers. There is nothing more we can do physically for you, but here is a list of people you can talk to if you feel you need to further down the line. The police also have good support networks. Do not be afraid to use them. Good luck.' He left us to get ready.

Susanna's parents had brought her some clothes and I borrowed them from her. Apart from that, we only had the cards and chocolates to put in a bag. I rang DCI Jones and told him we were ready.

Chapter 10

An hour later, the duty policeman came and escorted us down to the hospital entrance. As we stepped out in the air, we took a deep breath and held each other's hand. I couldn't help but look around suspecting everyone we saw as being a member of the gang.

The three of us got in the car. Jo wasn't there and I felt a sudden pang of fear. I counted to ten and calmed myself down.

The drive to the apartment block was surreal. I felt like a stranger in my own world. Susanna was squeezing my hand hard so I could tell she was feeling anxious too.

Arriving at the block, the police officer went first to check everything was okay and came back to collect us. Escorting us up the stairs, it all felt familiar, but it no longer felt like home. At the top of the stairs, Jo stood, and we both sighed a sigh of relief.

We headed inside the apartment, and I was relieved to see there were extra bolts on the door as well as the new locks. I slowly walked around checking if anything had changed, but, as far as I could tell, it looked the same. I looked at the bookshelf and felt my legs go weak. Jo and Susanna grabbed me and led me to a chair. I thought I was going to die; I couldn't get my breath. Jo brought me a glass of water.

'Try to breathe,' she instructed.

Eventually, I felt able to talk. 'There is a gap on the bookshelf where two books used to be. They are the books they brought to me when I asked for books. This means they were here. They must have used my keys. I don't know if I can stay here. It doesn't feel safe any more.'

Jo held my hand, reassuring me she would remain with us for as long as she could.

'I did some shopping for you and cleaned out your fridge. Can I get you anything to eat or drink?' she asked.

I pointed to a cupboard. 'There is a bottle of vodka in there. I will have a large one and I am sure Susanna would like one too.'

Jo brought the vodka and two glasses. 'I can't drink while on duty but carry on, you deserve it.'

With that, Susanna poured the largest vodka I had ever drank. By the time the bottle was empty, we both staggered to the bedroom and collapsed across the bed. Jo followed us in and covered us with a blanket. As she went to turn the light out, we both shouted, 'NO, leave it on.'

Chapter 11

In the morning, I woke up, wondering where I was. As my brain began to realise I was in my bedroom, my body relaxed. Susanna was still asleep. I crept out of the bedroom, pulling my gown around me. There was no sign of Jo in the living room, just a pillow and rolled up sleeping bag. I read the note she had written.

'I have to go into the office for a while, but I should be back by lunchtime. PO Andy Gray is on duty outside your front door. If you are worried about ANYTHING, please speak to him.'

I looked out the spyhole in the door and could see the policeman sitting across the hall reading a newspaper.

Putting the coffee machine on, I stood resting on the worktop thinking about the events of the past weeks and what the next few weeks would hold.

There was a knock on the door. Looking through the spyhole, I could see the policeman standing there. I opened the door as far as the chain would go.

'Yes.'

'Sorry, miss, to disturb you, but can I use your facilities?'

I let him in. While he was in the bathroom, Susanna came out of the bedroom sleepy-eyed and groaning. I put a coffee in front of her. She let out a scream and dropped the coffee when the policeman appeared. We sat her down and I poured coffee for all of us. The policeman went outside, apologising as he closed the door behind him. I quickly bolted and chained the door.

Susanna calmed down, and we talked about how we would

spend the day. I put the TV on and we watched a film. Jo arrived at lunchtime with fish and chips.

'I don't expect you ate breakfast, so I brought these. Nothing like good old fish and chips for comfort food.'

No one disagreed with her, and we tucked in enjoying the flavour.

Jo asked if we would like to go for a walk, but Susanna shook her head. As I was still taking it easy on my feet, we decided to wait a day or two. And so that is how the next couple of days went: sleeping, eating and watching TV.

Chapter 12

On the third day, I encouraged Susanna to shower and dress so we could go to a local café for our first outing. I felt I had to put a brave face on it as she was very nervous. Jo had to be at the station. PO Andy said that he would come with us.

It took us a while to get ready and build up the courage to leave the apartment. Locking the door behind us, we set off down the stairs. Andy went first and checked outside to make sure no one was watching us.

As we left the building, I noticed the police car was not in sight. 'Where is it?' I asked Andy.

'I'm not sure. I will check.' He radioed the car and after a few minutes, he got a reply.

'It's okay, they went to get more petrol as they were running low; I've told them where we will be and they will catch us up.'

With relief, we headed on down to the café at a slow pace. It was lovely to breathe the fresh air and feel free. We linked arms as if we were afraid that if we were apart one of us would disappear. Andy followed behind and we kept glancing back to make sure he was there.

Reaching the café, we looked through the window. There were only two other people sitting and chatting. It looked safe so we went in.

We got a table near the window where we could look out. We saw a police car pull up outside and although we could not see who was in it, we relaxed knowing it was there.

There was one waitress, so Andy said he was going to the gents and would order us drinks on the way. The man from the other table got up and followed him. I nudged Susanna and pointed out that the man had gone to the gents after the PO, and the woman had dropped her head down, so we were unable to see her face. Looking at each other, we couldn't help but be suspicious. The man came back and sat down but there was no sign of Andy the PO. Where was he?

The door of the café opened, and a man came in. He showed us his warrant card and introduced himself as DI Kennard. I relaxed and was about to ask him to check on Andy when he spoke. 'I'm sorry, ladies, but you will have to come with us. We have word that something is going down with the gang, and we need to get you back home. Go out to the car and wait; I will get your drinks.'

'What about Andy – the policeman who came with us?' we asked.

'Don't worry about him. While the drinks are being made, I will go up and tell him. He can walk back. Hurry up; we don't want to hang about.'

We grabbed our things and headed out to the car. Checking there was no one lurking, we almost dived into the car. Susanna had her phone out, looking at it. 'There's no messages from Jo on here; that's strange,' she muttered, looking at me.

I looked out the car window and noticed the man and woman who had been at the other table talking to DI Kennard. I thought it strange that they seemed to know each other.

DI Kennard got in the car with two bottles of Coke and straws. He handed one to each of us.

'Straws? Coke? Where's the hot chocolate?' we asked.

'I didn't think you ladies would wish to spill anything on

your clothes, which is why I put straws in. The hot chocolate was taking too long to make. Drink up; you must be thirsty.' He looked at us strangely.

Not wanting to appear ungrateful, we drank. I thought it tasted a bit strange, but Susanna had almost finished hers and said she didn't notice anything.

Susanna leaned forward. 'What about Andy? Did you tell him?'

I looked at her; she was beginning to slur her words.

The DI gave a sneer. 'Well, you know yourself, Susanna, strange things can happen in toilets.'

Chapter 13

By now, I was starting to feel lightheaded. I fumbled for my phone, but my eyes were too blurred, and my hands lost their grip on it. I watched it drop to the floor in slow motion. It was then that I saw, as my body lurched forward, the driver had blonde hair showing on his collar. I felt the straw being pushed into my mouth and the command, 'DRINK', before everything began to fade into darkness.

When I woke up, it was dark. I could see some pinpricks of light high above my head. The stench was unbearable, and I lifted my top up over my mouth.

'Susanna, are you there?'

A voice came out of the darkness. 'She is still out of it.'

'Who are you? What do you want?' I asked, even as my brain began to tell me I was a prisoner again.

'My name is Kellie,' came the reply. 'We are in a big metal room. There are ten of us, and, with you, it's twelve. We have no idea how long we have been here or why we are here. We haven't seen anyone. They just throw in bottles of water and sandwiches. All we can do is sleep. Some of us are very weak, and there is not much air.'

I felt a wave of despair come over me. There was nothing I could do except hope that someone saw us being lifted from the car.

I heard a groan and Susanna stirred. 'Rachel, Rachel, are you here?'

'Yes.' I padded my hand around, trying to find her. I pulled it back with a gasp, as I felt something very cold. I didn't want to think what it was, but, as I hesitantly reached out again and touched it, gently running my hand along it, I realised it was human. I shook it but nothing happened. Pulling back, I reached to the other side of me and found Susanna. She grasped my hand.

'Did you press the button on the phone?' she whispered.

'I am so sorry; I dropped it before I could.' I sobbed. She did not reply.

'Susanna, Susanna, are you all right?' I pushed at her. She did not respond. I tried to get up but there was not enough space, so I rolled towards her and grabbed her.

'Susanna, wake up, please,' I begged. She still felt warm but there did not seem to be any movement and I could only hope she had gone back to sleep.

I began to cry. Other voices came from the darkness trying to comfort me, but it felt like there was no hope for any of us.

Chapter 14

I asked the others who they were and had they heard anything to indicate how long they would be kept for.

Kellie seemed to be the spokesperson. She related what she could, which wasn't much. They, like Susanna and me, could remember nothing of how they came to be where they were. Most of them were teenagers between the ages of fifteen and seventeen, with a couple being older. She could say that they thought the men were foreign. One spoke as though he was Eastern European. They mentioned Amsterdam, Poland, Belarus and Russia. They were guessing they would be taken abroad and used as sex workers.

I couldn't bring myself to tell them what I knew. I told them I thought it was for slavery in rich people's houses. All the time they had hope that it could be for something else; it would give them strength.

The light through the holes dimmed, and no one had brought water or food. The floor was hard, and I was beginning to shiver with the cold.

I curled up beside Susanna, wrapping my arms around her to try and keep us both warm. I could feel hot tears on my cheeks as I drifted off to sleep.

Suddenly, I was awoken by a loud bang. I could hear the others whimpering and shuffling around trying to get as far away from the door as they could. Light was streaming through the holes, so I knew it was daytime again.

The door crashed open, and we screamed, turning our eyes away from the bright light.

'It's okay, it's okay, you are safe; we are police,' came a voice.

'Jo,' I called.

'Rachel, thank goodness! Listen, everyone, I have sunglasses here; put them on before you open your eyes again. They will help with the brightness.'

'Where are we?' some asked.

'You are in an old shipping container.'

Then I heard her gasp. 'Oh no! You better get these girls out of here and forensics in as soon as possible.'

Putting the glasses on, I opened my eyes and was horrified at the scene around me. Women and girls sat huddled together. Some of them looked very young. They were unkempt, scared and dirty. Empty water bottles and sandwich packets were strewn around. The bucket for sanitary use was overflowing. It was a wonder any of them had survived. They were being encouraged to go to the door and be helped outside but it was clear that some of them were in a state of shock. I looked to either side of me and saw the body of a very young girl curled up as though sleeping, but she was clearly dead. I felt anger rise in me.

Worse was to come when I went to Susanna. She looked like she was sleeping; her blonde hair spread out around her, but her lips were blue. I shook her hard. She felt very cold and didn't respond. I rested my head on her and sobbed until I was lifted away and taken out of the container.

As I was helped outside, a blanket was thrown around my shoulders and I held it tight. As my eyes became accustomed to the light, I removed the glasses.

Police were everywhere. Ambulances were in a line and the

girls were being led to them. A police canteen van arrived, and I hoped it would have warm food for us all.

Standing against one of the police cars were two men handcuffed to two policemen. The one who had said he was a DI and the blonde man.

A burning rage took over me as I lunged towards them and could hear myself screaming, 'MURDERERS!' I wanted to kill them.

Jo grabbed me and pulled me back. Leading me away, I watched the other girls being given a mug of something then helped into ambulances and driven away.

I looked at Jo. 'I was stupid; I didn't listen to my gut telling me something was wrong. By the time I did, I was unable to press the emergency button on the phone; I dropped it – it's my fault Susanna is dead.'

'No, you mustn't think that. Susanna managed to press hers, probably as you left the café. She was very nervous so probably thought it wouldn't matter to be careful. It took us a while to find you, as the trackers went offline not long after you were abducted. Taking a chance, we came back to the warehouse where we had caught the first man and brought the dogs with us. There, we found your phones, so we hoped you would be close by. But as you can see there are a lot of containers here, and we were not even sure if you were in one or had already been moved. As we were searching, we caught Blondie and his mate trying to get away. They refused to talk, so we had to continue using the dogs. Eventually, the dogs led us here and knowing the game was now up, they handed over the keys, and you know the rest.'

I looked at the container and back at the men. How could they do this to anyone? I screamed at them again, calling them every name that I could think of. I couldn't stop and knew I was becoming hysterical. A medic came over and told me to swallow a couple of pills with the hot cup of soup he handed me.

Jo had her arms around me to comfort me, and it was then I noticed how much I smelled. It was making me feel sick.

I asked if I could go home and give a statement the next day. I just wanted to get in a hot shower and wash the dirt and smells off and then snuggle down in my own bed and shut out the world. Nothing would be the same again.

Jo signalled a policeman and instructed him to drive me home and stay with me.

When I arrived home, the first thing I saw was some of Susanna's clothes. I broke down and lifted a jumper to my face crying into it. The policeman handed me a coffee and urged me to sit down but I headed to the bathroom and got into a very hot shower. With my hair washed and the smells gone, I held Susanna's jumper and curled up in bed. The pills must have worked as I was more relaxed and drifted off to sleep.

The light through the window of the bedroom woke me and I lay there for a while before getting up. It was noon.

As I went into the living room, there was a knock on the door. The young policeman opened it, and DCI Jones came in. He looked as worn out as I felt. Wrapping my cardigan tightly around me, I curled up on the couch.

'How are you? Did you sleep okay?' I nodded.

He continued, 'We have rescued ten girls/women including you. One young girl died, but we don't know why yet, and it is thought that Susanna had a stroke brought on by the anxiety and stress of the kidnap, but we will know more when the post-mortem results are released.' He took a breath and asked if we could have a drink before we carried on. I looked at the policeman and said he could make them and told him where to find the biscuits.

'Please continue, DCI Jones. I need to know everything.'

'Okay. Well, we caught the three men here as you know. We thought it would be a bigger gang but, being just the three, it is probably why they got away with it for so long. There weren't enough leads. That nurse spotting you was the breakthrough we were all waiting for. The Dutch have arrested a bigger gang over there including women. They also rescued twenty girls who were being held on a farm. We do not have reports from other countries yet, but it is hoped that the chain will be broken. It seems that they have been trafficking girls and sometimes boys through Holland, Germany, Poland, Belarus, and then into Russia. It is a well-established route but now we have a way in. We are hopeful we can shut it down. In the meantime, we will be putting a case together, but this could take years. Once you have made your statement you will be able to get on with your life until it comes to court.'

'Did you catch the man and woman who were in the café?' I asked.

'Who?'

'Susanna and I had our suspicions that they were in on it because when PO Andy went to the gents, the man got up and followed him. He came back but Andy didn't. We did not have time to think about it before the fake policeman came in and urged us to leave quickly. Is Andy all right?'

DCI Jones looked perplexed and then angry. He immediately got on his phone and spoke to someone.

Hanging up, he said they would be checking CCTV in the area. He also said that PO Andy was okay. He couldn't remember anything much except that the couple did not look suspicious. He had a vague description but, hopefully, the CCTV would help.

I was glad to know that the PO was okay, but I felt a bit of panic realising that the two people had got away.

He handed me a list of phone numbers.

'These are victim support lines. Please use them as much as you want. They are there to help you through this. I will let you know as soon as we catch the other two.'

'Thank you,' I said. 'Thank you for not giving up on us or any of those girls.'

When DCI Jones left, the young policeman went with him and the apartment suddenly felt empty.

Chapter 15

I locked the door behind them and having a look out of the window to ensure no one was watching the apartment, I began folding up Susanna's clothes to give to her parents. I threw all mine in the bin.

I left all the lights on and paced up and down, trying to work out what I would do.

I felt an inner rage and grabbing cleaning materials I set to and cleaned the apartment from top to bottom.

I phoned Susanna's parents and offered my condolences which sounded hollow even to my ears. I asked if I could go to her funeral and maybe meet with them for a coffee. They were pleased and agreed. It would be good to learn more about Susanna and what her life had been like.

I phoned my job and told them I was taking a month off to recover and then I booked a flight to Spain to visit a friend and hopefully relax.

The journey through the airport was horrendous. Every foreign voice I heard made me jump. I found myself checking on where the security guards were standing. I was glad to reach my friend and feel safe.

While I was away, Jo phoned me to let me know the cause of Susanna's death.

She had been given too much of the drug used to sedate us and it caused her death by overdose. The men were now being charged with murder for the death of both Susanna and the young girl who had been beside me in the container. They were also being charged with kidnap, unlawful imprisonment, and anything else the police could come up with. The police also had leads on the couple from the café and they were being followed up.

I felt sadness at the waste of life caused by these evil people. I sat on the beach watching the sun set and thought about Susanna and her last moments. She had been a beautiful young girl destroyed by evil.

The rest of the month went by quickly and I returned home on a miserable damp day. The taxi dropped me off and with trepidation I entered the building and then my apartment. Turning on the lights, I sighed with relief to see it looked the same and the threads I had put across the apartment in various places were still there. None of them were broken. No one had been in.

Making coffee and sitting on the couch, I rang Susanna's parents. The funeral was the next day. There would not be many people, but they wanted to spend some time with me afterwards.

I rang DCI Jones to let him know I was back. He informed me that all the defendants had pleaded guilty to all charges, and I would not have to go to court. The couple from the café had been arrested and would be charged with kidnap and anything more they found as the investigation went on. The European police had not only broken the gang in Holland but also in Germany and Poland. The Belarus government was reluctant to do anything, and it was feared that that link would remain. However, he was hopeful that some of the police would be able to work behind the scenes and destroy it in their own way!

I was speechless with relief. Feeling weak, I was just about to hang up when his voice interrupted me, 'Are you still there, Rachel?'

'Yes,' I whispered.

'It's over; you can try to move on.'

I wondered how I would ever be able to move on. When would the fear and nightmares stop?

'Rachel?'

'Yes.'

'As you are no longer required as a witness, would you like to go for a meal sometime?'

I smiled; maybe with his help, the future would be brighter and maybe just maybe when I am feeling stronger, I could get a job helping other girls and women who have been through the same ordeal. I felt I owed it to Susanna so she would never be forgotten.